OLD NORM

OLD NORM

~

by
Tim Brown

RESOURCE *Publications* • Eugene, Oregon

OLD NORM

Resource Publications
An Imprint of Wipf and Stock Publishers
199 W. 8th Ave., Suite 3
Eugene, OR 97401

www.wipfandstock.com

PAPERBACK ISBN: 978-1-5326-8115-8
HARDCOVER ISBN: 978-1-5326-8116-5
EBOOK ISBN: 978-1-5326-8117-2

Manufactured in the U.S.A.   03/14/19

This book is dedicated to my wife, Barbara,
and my daughters, Heather and Megan, who taught me
that we are, indeed, connected to people in ways that
we cannot imagine.

Contents

1

~

Disagreeable Generosity

We are called to love our neighbors and Dad said that means all of them, not just the ones we choose. Of course, in a town as small as Spring Valley, Nebraska, everyone is your neighbor, even Old Norm. His full name was Norman E. Benton. We never learned what the E. stood for and that didn't matter much. We just called him Old Norm. He was a hard neighbor to love and, for our family, even harder to avoid. At least, that's the way it seemed to me when my older brother, Mike, moved back from Omaha. Mike was a welder. He and his wife, Molly, lived in Omaha for about three years while he was learning his trade. Mike took a job as a contract welder with the Spring Valley Gas Company and our family was reunited. I was glad they were home. I was also extremely surprised when he agreed to a job interview with Old Norm.

Norman E. Benton was an important man in Spring Valley. He was rich, sometimes generous, and almost always insulting. When he did something nice, it always had a hook, like the time he bought the entire Spring Valley marching band new uniforms and then demanded that they carry his company flag right alongside the Stars and Stripes during the Founder's Day parade. Of course, we all enjoyed the party he threw after the parade. All the floats and folks wound up at his place for roasted pig, watermelon, and nonstop bluegrass music, all at Norm's expense. Still, people remembered him for his disagreeable behavior more than his conspicuous generosity. He owned a farm implement dealership and a huge country home on an 80-acre farm just south of town. He and his wife, Ruth, and two black Labs lived there unassumingly, except when he threw a party.

In person, Norman E. Benton was a loud and bad-tempered man. Dad likened him to a hand grenade because, once you hear him, it is too late. Old Norm's wealth was the persistent footing beneath all his human relationships. His wife seemed to enjoy being rich, without being snobbish. People liked her, even though nobody knew her very well. Dad said she didn't sit still long enough to let anyone get to know her. There was a nervous haste about her that hindered familiarity. She always seemed so busy, so preoccupied by some unknown, important task. People just didn't want to bother her with small talk. No one had the chance, or took the chance, to find common ground with Ruth Benton. From her hurried footsteps to her quick-flash smile, which was gone before you were sure she'd given it to you, Ruth Benton was an enigma. Mom was sympathetic. She thought the poor woman had just never learned to relax. Dad called her a fart in a skillet. He had a mental satchel full of pithy one-liners.

Despite her jittery temperament, Ruth seemed as dutiful to Norm as his two black dogs. Of course, the dogs didn't care about his money like we all did. It was the reason we all felt so special when he was kind to us. It was also part of the reason we hated him when he resumed his habitual nastiness, which he always did. He could be a foul and disagreeable man, and his face matched his personality, especially his smile. When he smiled, the corners of his mouth turned down rather than up. The result was a mischievous sneer and, even with a full belly laugh behind it, it gave you pause.

One day, behind his disconcerting grin, Norm told Armando Reyes that he should go on back to Mexico where he could find a sombrero to sleep under. Armando was a mechanic who worked for Norm. He missed a day of work because of illness, which Norm thought gave him the right to needle him. Another time, when he bumped into Mom at the grocery store, his sting landed a little closer to home. He asked Mom what sort of work my Dad was doing these days. My dad changed jobs a lot. Norm was a master at finding and exploiting personal vulnerabilities to make people squirm.

Unexpectedly, Norm called and asked Mike to visit him at his dealership to talk about a job. Mike was four years my senior. I idolized him. Our common experience with Norm was based mostly on small-town gossip and our parent's quiet acknowledgment that Old Norn was someone to avoid if you could. I figured that Mike had forgotten about Norm's reputation for meanness when he accepted Norm's invitation.

Norm welcomed him home with a handshake and a slap on the back and his mischievous, inverted smile. "So, you are a welder," Norm said. "That's good. That's good. That's far more than your father ever did. Damn, how many jobs has he had now, anyway?"

Half embarrassed and half angry, my brother answered, "I don't know."

Our father truly was a jack-of-all-trades and a master of none. He sold fertilizer, dug wells, drove a hay truck, engraved tombstones, and painted houses, just to name a few of his many professional stops. Many times, job hopping can be chalked up to alcohol abuse or a short temper or some other human hobgoblin. Such was not the case with Dad. He'd just get bored and move on. Because he was smart and likable and an extremely hard worker, he did well at each of his jobs. He was not a shirker. He would simply lose interest. I think Mom found quiet reassurance in his professional fickleness. Though I doubted her sincerity, she used to say that she was afraid he'd finally find something that held his interest and run off and leave us. He'd just smile at her and say, "Fear is a wish, Mom. Fear is a wish."

Just like we knew how rich Norm was, everyone knew how smart and capable Dad was. I think that's what stuck in Norm's craw about him. He just couldn't understand how someone could be so smart and yet so willing to just slog along on the uncertain margins of success and prosperity. Or, maybe he didn't care at all about Dad and was just having a good time making Mike uncomfortable.

2

∽

The Challenge

Mike was surprised and annoyed at Old Norm's biting words of welcome, but he remained curious enough to stay with the conversation a bit longer. Norm got right to the point. "I need a welder, Mike. Let's see what you can do." Norm tossed Mike a tobacco tin and asked him to cut it in half and then weld it back together. The thin metal of the pocket-sized tobacco tin was easy to cut, but it would be a challenge to weld.

Mike thought it was odd that he was asked to demonstrate his welding skill before he had even shown interest in the job, but it was a challenge too appealing to turn down. He examined the Sir Walter Raleigh tobacco tin carefully and suppressed a smile. He had welded thin tin before in friendly competition with coworkers at his Omaha job, but he certainly wasn't going to tell Norm about that.

"You still rolling your own?" Mike kidded.

"Nope. Don't smoke. My daddy did though. That's the last tobacco tin I have to remember him by. So, don't cut it if you can't put it back together," Norm said, not returning Mike's smile.

Mike knew he was lying, but he played along. He studied the little red can harder than was necessary. He pressed its flexible sides with great care and ran his index finger up and down the edge seam at least three times. He flipped open the loosely hinged lid and snapped it shut with authority. "Sure, I can do that," he said, dropping his act of reluctance with a self-assured grin. "I'll get my stuff. It's in the truck."

"No. You will use my stuff," Norm demanded.

"Gee, Norm. If I was putting a trailer hitch on your Jeep, I'd gladly use your equipment. But this requires surgical precision. It's delicate work. I'll need to use my own stuff."

"Okay, have it your way."

"You can get me a bucket of water, though. Appreciate it."

They walked to Norm's workshop, and Mike cut the can in half with a pair of tin snips rather than the acetylene torch. He wanted the edges to be clean and straight. It was a slow process because he had to use low heat. He had to weld a little, stop the weld, skip ahead a fraction of an inch, and start again and weld a little more. Stopping the weld and skipping ahead allowed the metal to cool so that it didn't melt away. The recurrent breaks in the weld required him to round the can twice, first with a partial weld and then with a second round to fill in the gaps. It was tedious work and it took him over 20 minutes to reattach the can halves with a thin, even bead.

Mike removed his welder's mask, stuck a screwdriver into the open tin and held it up hot for Norm's quick inspection before he dropped it in the water bucket. It chirped as it fell into the cold water. That was the successful conclusion to Mike's welding demonstration for Old Norm and the beginning of an unruly relationship that captivated us all. "There you are. I think your daddy would be happy about that," Mike kidded.

Norm fished the cooled tobacco tin out of the water and examined it closely. He raised his eyebrows, smiled, and said, "Nice work. Very nice. Yes, Daddy would be pleased. So, would yours, I think. You know what I mean. You've found one thing and become damned good at it. Sure isn't your daddy's way, is it? How many jobs did you say he had?"

I've noticed that when people move away from a place for a little time, they think differently when they return. It isn't so much that they think they are better or smarter because they've been away. It is just that they sometimes forget about the way of things in their old place. I think Mike had forgotten how quickly Old Norm could get under your skin.

The wound was fresh, and he remembered. He was mad . . . smart mad. He had that ability. He could be absolutely steamed, and you'd never know it. He'd just let his anger slip into the situation like a silent, well-thrown javelin. Mike secretly simmered as the reconstructed tobacco tin lay unceremoniously on the work bench.

"My dad has had a lot of jobs. He also has a lot of friends," Mike responded. "How you doing on friends, Norm? You got anybody to talk to besides those two old black dogs over there." Mike's smile belied the depth of his anger.

"Those two dogs are better company than most people."

"But they don't give a crap about all your money. How can you possibly enjoy them?"

"Do you want the job or not?" Norm abruptly dodged the javelin.

"Are you offering me a job?"

"Yes. I like your spunk. If you promise not to be like your old man and run off after the next bright and shiny thing, I'll beat what you're making now by 20 percent.

"So, what would I do, weld a few tobacco tins or just sit around and be spunky?"

"You know, I think the day your daddy sat you down to teach you manners he got bored and moved on to something else, didn't he? When can you start? I got three disc blades that need mending and a combine header with a torn housing.

Mike was back into the hometown swing of things. Getting there did not take long. Norm's nastiness was no longer just small-town gossip with a casual nod from Mom and Dad. It was real. Rubbing up against it surprised you, like the little chill you feel when a spiderweb catches the hair on your arm. As creepy as it is, you know there is no real reason to panic, but you still brush it off and move on as quickly as you can. Mike would resist becoming a full-time employee of Norm's, and I think his refreshed memory of Norm's belittling nature calmed him down a little.

He may have even recognized the hidden value of nasty Old Norm. Mike remembered all the sarcastic fun we had talking about Old Norm. He wasn't just fair game for kids. Vicariously, our parents participated. They watched and smiled. On rare occasions, they offered an alternate adult perspective. Old Norm was a common thread that connected us all. He shortened the distance between child and parent, neighbors and neighbors, teachers and students, shop keepers and customers, and preachers and congregants. When Pastor Weber talked about forgiveness, we all suspected that Old Norm was lurking somewhere in the back of his mind.

"Tell you what. I'm just a contract welder for the gas company. That means I can also be a contract welder for you. I can start on that stuff first thing in the morning, providing you pay me what I'm worth." Mike liked the thought of having Old Norm owing him a little something now and again.

3

~

The Entertainer

Norm would rather have had Mike directly under his thumb, but he did need a welder. They eventually came to terms and Mike's new arm's-length relationship with Norm worked out well. Mike made a little extra money and, more important to us, we all had a steady supply of new Old Norm stories to keep us entertained. I am sure that we shared them with folks who we would never have connected with without him. That's not to suggest that Mike didn't get downright mad at Norm's insulting behavior at times. He did. One day he asked Mike why he had ever moved back from Omaha. "What was the matter?" he asked. "Couldn't you cut it on your own in the big city?"

I don't know why that made Mike so angry. Maybe there was a spot of truth in what Norm said. Of course, Mike knew that insensitive remarks were always going to be part of the Norm Benton terrain. Whatever the reason, on that day, Mike had reached his insult quota. He said nothing to

Norm, but when he got home, he grumbled aloud for about half an hour. After he cooled down, I confessed to him that I feared he might lose his cool someday and hurt Norm, maybe burn him bad with his welding torch or something worse.

He looked at me with his smart-mad grin and gave me one of Dad's pat answers, "Fear is a wish, Brother. Fear is a wish."

Welding suited my brother just fine. He loved to work with his hands, and he loved to compete. That's why he was so prepared for Norm's tobacco-tin challenge. I, on the other hand, had a hard time learning to tie my shoes. As far as manual dexterity was concerned, he had me beat hands down. When it came to using tools and completing manual chores, I did just what I had to do, nothing more. And his off-the-cuff responses to Norm's insults were far more than I could muster. In more purely cerebral pursuits, I did better. Mike said I was a brooding worry wart. Mom said I was extremely thoughtful. I suppose they both were right. But it was true that I could agonize over a problem for a long time before solving it or letting it go. Our differences were a fine thing, really. They gave us both a chance to appreciate one another in a totally non-competitive way.

We fussed some, but we never fought. Because he was older, he automatically had teasing rights. He teased. I fussed. Mom listened. We learned early that there was no easier way to trigger her bad-behavior alarm than to speak maliciously. Even playful banter was not allowed if it held a hint of meanness. "Tame your tongues," she'd snap. "A sharp tongue dulls a caring heart." It took me a while to understand what she meant, but it was clear that what came out of my mouth mattered a great deal to her. By the time Mike returned from Omaha, our bantering days were all but over. But neither of us ever forgot Mom's sensitivity to harsh, spiteful words. That's why we usually kept our responses to Norm's unpleasantness on the lighter side. He was the one, after all, whose caring heart would be dulled beyond repair.

4

∾

Change

Having Mike and Molly home felt correct. They were married just out of high school. They were perfect together then. They were perfect together when they returned home. They moved in with us until they could find a place of their own. I was glad they did. Being around them triggered a familiar and comfortable certainty, and it was welcome in a time of national and personal uncertainty. Their presence seemed to hold the disorder spawned by the Vietnam War at bay for a while. It was 1968 and the war raged on and war protests grew louder and louder. We had uncertainty with our coffee every morning. Military duty was almost a foregone conclusion for a single, twenty-something male in good health.

Mike's marriage kept the draft board away. I would have a college deferment for a time. Oddly, even after I graduated, I was not drafted.

Molly's brother wasn't so lucky. A year or so after living through the Tet Offensive of 1968, he committed suicide. No one knew for sure what caused him to take his own life, but Molly blamed it on his decision to extend his stay in Vietnam after the first year. Most soldiers who made it through one year went home feeling lucky. After a two-week stateside leave, Molly's brother went back for more. Six months into his second tour he shot himself. News of a suicide is always numbing. It makes no sense. It mocks hope. It dilutes grief with anger, confusion, and guilt. It was especially baffling to Molly. She knew her brother was shy and lacked confidence, but he seemed to have finally found himself in the Army. She took extraordinary pride in his military service. Now, he was a wartime casualty. But his suicide was the reason no one talked about his death very much, and that is probably the reason that Norm Benton didn't give a second thought to droning on about his position on the war in front of Mike.

Norm was a die-hard hawk who thought carpet bombing Hanoi was totally justified and the hippy freaks who were protesting the war should be jailed as traitors. It was as though his nastiness had found a new home in wartime politics. His political positions were cast in stone and he never missed an opportunity to tell you about them. Mike continued to weld for Norm two days a week, and there was usually enough work to do that Mike could hide behind his welding mask and avoid the acidic, political harangues that were becoming habitual for Norm. There was a time, however, when Mike had to put on his smart-mad face and bring Norm up short.

It was payday. Norm brought Mike his check and Mike took off his mask and gloves to receive it. "Here you go, Mike," Norm said. "You do good work. I'll bet if you had joined the Army you would have gone over there and welded shut the whole damned Ho Chi Minh Trail. Good thing you got married, huh? What about your brother? Scott, isn't it? He still in college?"

"Sure is. And still on scholarship. He got the brains. I got the blowtorch," Mike responded, smiling and a bit surprised that Old Norm knew my name.

"Well, he'll get his chance in about a year or two. You can be sure we'll still be fighting those gook commies by then. Christ's sake, I wish we'd try to win this thing. Seems to me we're just pissing away our chances to win. Hell, everybody goes over for a year. Then they come home and act half-embarrassed for having been there or they act half-crazed and want to be treated like war heroes. And they haven't done crap."

That was too close to home for Mike. Molly was still mourning her loss. It hurt him terribly to watch Molly suffer.

"You ever go to war, Norm?" Mike asked.

"No. I was too young for the big one and Korea just sort of slipped right by me. Wasn't much of a war anyway."

"Ever even serve in the military?"

"Nope."

"You ever lost anybody to a war, Norm?"

"No. Why the interrogation, Mike. You one of those hippy protesters?"

"Do you know my wife, Norm?"

"Sure. Molly, isn't it?"

"She lost her brother in Nam six months ago. Do you want to tell her that he didn't do crap?"

"Well, no, of course not. I was just sayin' . . ."

"That's your problem, Norm. Once you start talking you don't know when to stop. Think what you want about the war, but keep it to yourself, okay? What is it you want, Norm? You want me to sign a petition? You want me to nominate you for President? You want me to tell everyone how smart you are? Here's what I'd tell them, Norm. I would tell them that I like you, but you talk too much for your own good. I'll be back next week, if you want me here. However, I will not be here if you are going to carry on about the war. Call me when you decide." Mike picked up his mask and gloves and walked to his pickup.

Mike's arms-length relationship with Norm allowed him to quit Norm without hesitation. As an independent, part-time welder he was free to work or not to work. He knew it and Norm knew it, but this was the first time he had demonstrated how easy it was to disengage from Norm's frail grasp. He had a cautious fondness for Norm but was relieved that his escape strategy had worked so well.

Norm called him on the following Monday. His apology was quick but uncommonly reflective for Norm.

"Mike, I'm sorry if I offended you. Sometimes I get carried away. At home, Ruth reins me in from time to time. I guess I should also depend on guys like you to be my barometer."

"Barometer?" responded Mike. "More like a wind gauge, don't you think?"

Norm was silent for a moment. Then, it was back to business. "Now, Rufus DeWitt brought in his baler. Needs the bale chute mended. Will I see you tomorrow?

Mike wasn't ready to let Norm off the hook. "Did you read the sports page this morning?" he asked.

"No."

"Go ahead. Read it. Read it tomorrow, too. Then we can talk about football and the price of season tickets rather than the war." Mike instructed. "Deal?"

Mike imagined Norm swallowing hard before he answered. "Sure. I'll see you tomorrow."

So, Mike went back to work for Norm after reinforcing the boundaries of their relationship. Mike explained it to me this way, "Every good welder knows that you shouldn't get too close to the flame." Clearly, he was glad that he had put Norm in his place.

Bad news demanded that he reconsider how close to Norm he wanted to stand. About three weeks later, Mike went to the dealership early on Tuesday morning. He was alone in the front office examining the list of welding jobs scheduled for the day when Norm called with the news about his wife.

Ruth Benton's brisk pace was permanently slowed one cold Friday morning when she slipped on the icy Post Office steps. She cracked her head on the steel handrail as she went down. She lost consciousness and died the next day. It was a death that came as a sudden, unexpected loss that required some pondering. It came down to this: We would miss her jittery, fleeting presence, but not her. To be sure, there was no spontaneous outpouring of sympathy for Old Norm. Those that did feel the need to express concern found a safe way to do it, one that wouldn't make them seem insincere and one that would allow them to avoid the embarrassment of seeing a hard man mourn. In fact, it was hard to imagine him grieving. We didn't want to. He was a valued fixture of contempt in our lives, and we didn't want to change that by recognizing his humanity. Still, we knew changes like death demand attention. Mom bought a card to send from the family, and she bought one for Mike to send on his own. Then, a day after her death, we received a surprising visit from Pastor Weber. Dad wasn't home from work yet, but the pastor wasn't looking for Dad. He asked to speak with Mike.

His request was simple but unusual. He wanted Mike to join him during his prefuneral visit. He knew that Mike worked for Norm, and he thought it would be a good idea to have someone with him during the visit who knew Norm better than he did. Norm was a Christmas and Easter Christian. Sometimes, not even that.

Mom and Mike sat on the couch. The pastor had Dad's big chair, and I pulled up the cushioned hassock next to the pastor so that I could be closer to the conversation. Mom's eyes burned a hole in my forehead as she gave her head a hard tilt toward the chair across the room. I moved to the chair.

"So, would you do it? You don't have to say a thing. Just be there. You'd be a tremendous help," said Pastor Weber.

Mike hesitated, rolled his eyes at me, and answered, "Pastor, I am a lot of things, but I am not what you would call a friend of Norm's, and I hardly knew his wife. I weld things for Norm. That's all I do. How could any of that possibly help you?

"Oh, it's not me you'd help. You'd help Norm."

"What?"

"You do talk to him some, don't you?

"Of course."

"Sure, you do, and they tell me that you can pretty much hold your own with Norm. You know, when he starts to needle you, you needle back, right?"

Some of our cynical Norm gossip had obviously made its way to the pastor.

"Respects your honesty, I'll bet." continued Pastor Weber. "But that's just part of it. The bigger deal is what you represent. You are Spring Valley. You are all the people in this community he has insulted, belittled, and angered. You are the throng of offended neighbors that he has created over the years. And you are his release valve."

"Release valve?"

"Yep. Left to his own devices, spontaneous grief will elude Norm because he is afraid to be vulnerable in front of any of us. Unless he grieves, I mean really grieves, he will hurt for a long time and become even more cantankerous than he already is. But, with you there, there's a chance he'll realize the real value of community. He'll do that because you, one of his often-offended neighbors, was kind enough to sit with him. You will be the nonjudgmental tipping point. You'll be an open gate to friends he didn't know he had. Hopefully, he'll relax his guard and accept the deeply fruitful grief that only occurs when you share it with others."

The pastor was selling hard. Mike knew it and sat quietly for a moment staring at his shoes. I thought he would object to becoming a surrogate object of compassion for Old Norm. I didn't think being nonjudgmental about Norman E. Benton was something that Mike could ever do. I was wrong. He looked up from his shoes and said, "Guess it wouldn't do for him to throw one of his parties about now, would it?"

"He needs people, but a party won't do. Will you help?"

"Sure. When do we go?"

Pastor Weber picked him up at nine o'clock the next morning. Mike shot me a tight-lipped smile as he went out the door and headed for the car. Mom stood to my right with her left hand on my shoulder as we stood behind the closed screen door and watched them leave. As they drove away, she squeezed my shoulder once and then turned slowly and retreated into the kitchen. I don't know for sure, but I think she cried. It seemed like Mike had grown up in a single, decisive moment. Mom said later that she thought the whole thing was a miracle. But it was Mike's miracle, not mine.

5

≈

Getting to Know Ruth

The meeting with Norm was surprisingly pleasant. Pastor Weber offered no explanation for Mike being there and Norm seemed not to question his presence. Mike didn't say much beyond his first hello. The three of them made their way through the well-appointed great room, with its prominent grand piano, and entered the cheerful country kitchen. Norm took a chair at the head of the kitchen table, nearest the freshly brewed coffee on the counter behind him. The pastor and Mike flanked him on opposite sides of the table. Norm retrieved the coffee pot, sat, and poured a cup for each of them without asking if they wanted any. Then he slid several pages from a yellow, legal-sized tablet across the table to Pastor Weber. The pastor had asked Norm to put some thoughts together about Ruth's life so he could prepare his remarks for the funeral. He did one better. He gave him ten hand-written pages about Ruth and their life together. Pastor Weber placed the document on the kitchen table before him and silently read. Except for the occasional coffee-pot gurgle and page-turn rattle, the kitchen was quiet. Mike reluctantly made eye contact with Norm and mouthed the words, "I'm sorry." Norm nodded his thank you. Pastor Weber continued to read. Minutes passed. Mike wondered why the pastor didn't wait until later to read Norm's notes and get on with the conversation. But it was an unexpected, giant step in Norm's grieving process and the pastor figured he owed it to Norm to give his written words immediate attention. Mike thought for a moment that Pastor Weber might be giving the unexplained presence of "tipping-point Mike" an exaggerated chance to sink in. Finally, Pastor Weber spoke.

"Thank you, Norm. You've pretty much done my work for me. She was a very interesting lady. I wish I had known her better."

"She could be a difficult person to get to know," responded Norm. "I think that's why we got along so well. She was so willing to go unnoticed and to play second fiddle, which sort of fit perfectly with my own hankering to be in charge. Truth be known, she was smarter than most of us and more in charge than I ever was."

Norm and Ruth met at a wedding in Colorado Springs back in 1954. Norm's niece married a wealthy real estate developer, and Norm was more than willing to make the trip to Colorado to see how the other half lived. He was handsome, fit, and socially competent, although in an unpolished small-town sort of way. This new comparatively opulent venue was a captivating place to him.

The ballroom was overflowing with people, music, and raucous laughter. As Norm entered the room, a wispy, determined girl rushed by him without excusing herself. She was attractive, quick, and disinterested in anything but her unannounced destination. He could not tell if she was fleeing something fearful or if she was charging forward with some great, deliberate purpose. He would soon learn that the only thing she feared was social insincerity, and remaining clear of it was her only great, deliberate purpose. A philandering father and a flighty, socialite mother had set her course, a course not toward what she wanted, but a path away from what she did not want. It was clear that she and Norm were from very different social strata, and she liked that. Even then, he and his inverted smile had developed a penchant for biting sarcasm that kept people at bay. She liked that too because it could protect her from the noisy, social shallowness that her parents so enjoyed. She abandoned her parent-imposed hope of becoming a concert pianist for a new life with Norm. They were married a year later and began their unusual and gossip-worthy lives in Spring Valley.

Now she was dead, and Mike was recruited to help Norm mourn. Inescapable circumstances usually demand change. Mike changed. Others, including me, took longer, but almost everyone quietly recognized the need for change. That was probably why there was a respectable crowd at the funeral. Pastor Weber did a wonderful job of filling in the blanks for us about Ruth. Then he reminded us of one of the Bible's admonitions that I've always wrestled with.

"The Bible tells us to give thanks in all circumstances," he said. "Today, while we mourn the loss of Ruth Benton, we give thanks for a very private, but very remarkable life well spent." He ended the service with a simple, but sweet, recording that Norm had made of Ruth playing "His Eye Is on the Sparrow" on her grand piano. We all knew her a little better after he spoke.

The church was packed. Even Peggy Stewart was there. My locker had been next to Peggy's in high school because of the alphabetical sequencing of our names. We met every morning, said hello, retrieved our books, slammed our locker doors, and went on our separate ways. She was a quiet, plain girl. Outside of the morning "Hello, Peggy," I never really paid much additional attention to her, but I did like her. She was an unassuming country girl and there was no reason to think of her in any other way. I was always polite and respectful, and I even tried to kid with her sometimes. She'd smile, but not say a word. Her lack of response stumped me because I didn't know any other way to start a conversation. It never occurred to me to ask her something about her plans, her next class, her family, or her opinion of our aging English teacher. So, it was three school years of pleasant good mornings, innocent smiles, and locker door slams that eventually altered the course of my life. It was nice to see her. I introduced her to Mike.

During the funeral service and the reception, Norm was as quiet and civil as anyone had ever seen him. Eventually, he backslid to his old ways, but it seemed like his stinger was a little less toxic. Mom said that she wasn't sure if Norm had changed or if we had.

After Ruth's funeral, Pastor Weber checked in on Norm on Sunday afternoons for three consecutive weeks. It was not his usual grief protocol. He was afraid that the small-town, follow-up assistance that would have been extended automatically to other members of the community in similar circumstances would not be forthcoming for Norman E. Benton. Pastor Weber was right. The church's Women's Circle brought the obligatory casseroles to his home the day after the funeral: one hot and two frozen. Beyond that, people kept their distance. No one called. No one offered practical help with household chores. It wasn't a lack of compassion that kept them away. It was fear. No one knew how to handle Norm on a good day, let alone at a time when he was grieving. On his third and final Sunday visit,

Pastor Weber asked him about the disorganized stack of unopened sympathy cards that cluttered his kitchen table.

"Are you going to open those?" Pastor Weber asked.

"I doubt it. I just figured they all say the same thing," Norm responded. "I been through them, though. I know who sent them."

"Did you read through Ruth's funeral guest book that I brought you?"

"Yes. Thank you for bringing it." Norm responded, offering no indication of his feelings about the significant turnout for Ruth's funeral.

"Almost all the people who attended will be glad to help you if you ask them. You know that, don't you?"

"I suppose I do," was Norm's indifferent response.

"Please don't be afraid to ask for help, Norm. It's been said that the key to happiness is to keep life comprised of things eighty percent familiar and twenty percent strange. I think now, that formula is going to be out of whack for a while. The strange portion will swell a bit. When it does, don't be afraid to ask for help."

"It will be an adjustment, no doubt," Norm said.

"Well, Norm, I won't bother your Sunday afternoons anymore, unless you need me. If you want to talk again or need anything at all, please call me," Pastor Weber said. He left Old Norm sitting at his kitchen table staring at the clutter of unopened sympathy cards before him. Eventually, he found a box for the sympathy cards and the funeral guest book and hired his mechanic's wife, Juanita Reyes, to do housekeeping chores two days a week, which did little to adjust his loneliness.

6

~

Peas and Mashed Potatoes

About a month after Ruth's funeral, Norm was back at work full time. Mike always parked behind the dealership and entered through the shop door. As he did, he saw Norm standing at the far end of the shop bay motioning to him to come up front. "Come sit with me a minute, Mike," he requested. Then he turned and went to his office, which had an interior window providing a view of the showroom. Mike followed with absolutely no idea what was on Norm's mind. At Norm's invitation, he sat in the chair in front of Norm's desk, which was usually occupied by Norm's customers as he closed the deal on a new farm implement. Today, Norm wasn't selling tractors. He closed the door and sat behind his desk, rocked back in his squeaky, overstuffed chair, and got right to the point.

"You going to be a welder all your life?" Norm asked.

"What?" Mike blurted.

"Why don't you help me manage this place? I need help and you need to look ahead a little bit. Give up your gas company job and come and help me full time. We could work you into the management stuff a little at a time so we don't shock the other guys with an unexpected move. At first, you would continue to weld, plus, you would work the front counter. That would give your natural leadership skills a chance to bubble up gradually. Truth is, you are smarter than all of them, you get along with people without being fooled, and it's an opportunity to expand your horizons a little bit."

He looked Norm straight in the eye, halfway expecting to see his upside-down grin reveal the teasing truth of his flippant offer. Norm didn't smile.

"Damn, Norm, where's this coming from?" Mike responded, his surprise undeniable. Being called a natural leader wasn't new to him. He always enjoyed hearing the words, but he instinctively knew what was at stake in Norm's offer: his coveted independence as a contract welder.

"Look, Ruth's passing has sort of changed things a little. As I mentioned before, every now and then Ruth would set me straight when I spoke out of turn. She didn't do it often, just when I said something 'patently mean and stupid,' as she put it. It made her shiver. She was usually right. Sort of like you when you spit my Vietnam conversation back in my face a while back. I am sorry. Now, you are not taking her place. That is not what I am saying. What I am saying is that I need help. I need smart people around me. Plus, I need to back off a little. I need to take it easy or at least try to. What do you think?"

"I am not sure what to think, Norm. I suppose you've figured out what you'd pay me?"

"You will like it," Norm smiled. "Let's call it a day. Give it some thought and we can talk again tomorrow."

"Tomorrow is Saturday, Norm. Do you want me to come in?"

"Oh, yeah. Saturday. You're here next Tuesday, right?"

"Right."

"Let's do it then. That's soon enough." Norm saw a customer enter the showroom and got up to greet him. "Think about it, Mike. We'll talk again on Tuesday."

Mike left the dealership early that day. He was anxious to get home. He didn't tell Norm that Molly was pregnant. He had told no one.

It was the first Sunday of spring break. I was home from school. Mike and Molly had found a little, starter home by then, but, as usual, they came over after church for a late breakfast. Sundays were family day, and this would be a family day to remember.

We were seated around the kitchen table and after Mike was done kidding me about being a no-account college kid, he said he had something to talk to us about and told us about Norm's tentative offer and how it had come about. He explained Norm's observations about his natural leadership abilities and his ability to help him manage the business. He explained that no compensation amount had been discussed but that Norm had made it all sound very inviting.

"Inviting?" Dad questioned, with a smile.

"Did you just say that you were considering working for Norman E. Benton full time?" I added. "I knew I should not have gone off to college, Mike. You need me here to help you maintain your equilibrium."

Mike winked and nodded, affirming my concern, and then took Molly's hand and watched her break into a foretelling smile. "There is something else," he said. "Molly is pregnant."

I thought Mom would explode. She began with sort of a choked-back giggle, which quickly became laughter and a high-pitched scream. She got up and circled the table so fast that she spilled her coffee. She didn't stop. She smothered Molly in a long, heartfelt embrace. Then moved on to Mike. Dad mopped up Mom's coffee with a dishcloth and smiled and smiled.

"How soon, how soon, how soon?" Mom questioned as she released Mike from her Momma Hug.

"In seven months," Molly answered.

"What fantastic news," Mom said. "How are you feeling, Molly?"

"So far, so good," she said through her radiant smile.

Dad tossed the soggy dishrag in the skink, sat down, and interrupted. "Sort of an odd way to tell us, don't you think? Sounds like you are letting your peas touch your mashed potatoes." That was Dad's way of telling us to deal with one thing at a time. It seemed to him that working for Norm and starting a family were not necessarily complementary thoughts. They should be dealt with separately. One was a lifelong commitment. The other was an incidental, transient circumstance that might serve the other or not.

"You are right, Dad. But I'm having a hard time separating them. Molly just told me for sure two weeks ago and then Norm lays his deal on me. I mean, everything seemed to happen at once," Mike explained.

"Tell me what Norm said again."

Mike reexplained his conversation with Norm, including Norm's admission that he sometimes talks too much.

"That is peculiar, but Norm is peculiar. It could be that his grief eased a little when he talked business," Dad contemplated. "It could be that once he put his sorrow on the shelf and started talking to you about business, he allowed himself to forget about Ruth's death for a moment. That is natural, I guess. The question is, did he mean what he said while he was taking his breather from the reality of the day? I guess you'll soon find out."

Mike nodded in agreement.

"One other thing, Mike," Dad continued. "Norm is what he is. I've known him a long time. He was two years ahead of me in high school. He was difficult then and he is difficult now. You cannot expect to change him. He may seem softer now in the wake of his wife's death, but he will always be contrary, insulting, and confusing. That you cannot change. All you can hope to change is the relationship. Look how much it has changed since you started welding for him. But, honestly, Mike, your flexibility and common sense caused that change, not his. See what he has to say, but if you cannot stomach his orneriness, leave it alone. I have worked with a lot of different people. Probably too many. But I have learned that you can't change people. All you can do is study the relationship and tweak it a little to try to make it better. So, if you work for Norm, there will always be a job within a job that you must accept as part of the territory. If you can spar with him and enjoy doing it, great. Do it. But, here's the truth: You can be a good dad with or without Norm."

Dad had separated the peas from the mashed potatoes. Of course, almost everyone quietly wondered whether we were seeing divine tumblers falling into place. Ruth's death, Norm's recognition that he needed qualified help, and Mike's status as an expectant father were oddly coincidental. Mom's response was not quite so cautious.

"Sometimes I think that there are no coincidences, Mike. Sometimes I think that we all think too hard about next steps. Sometimes they are scary. But we must take them just the same," Mom advised. "Like when you decided to go with Pastor Weber to visit Norm when Ruth died. You didn't hesitate. I was so proud. Of course, that decision is different than this one, but see what he has to offer and don't walk away from something good just because it requires you to do something that you are not entirely comfortable with at the time. Your dad is right, you can be a good dad with or without Norm, but there are times when the peas and the mashed potatoes are supposed to touch one another."

There it was: Mom's patient hope for more security and Dad's deep-seated dread of lost independence. It was the unspoken tension that we had grown up with. We knew it well. The chasm between the two most important people in our lives had opened before us, its edges very well defined. Mike glanced at me, then at Molly. I caught his glance and looked at Dad. He smiled faintly and shut his eyes in a long, deliberate blink. Mom stared at her hands, which surrounded her fresh cup of hot coffee.

Sometimes those on the periphery of a problem become more anxious and overwrought than those at the heart of it. Molly's calm, kind voice ended the conversation. She took Mike's hand and said, "He'll know what to do when the times comes. I am sure of that."

Mike's job status was in limbo, but his new focus was not. He was busy planning for a child, and he stopped feeding us Norm tales almost immediately after the funeral. Molly's pregnancy was part of it, but so was Norm. It was as though Norm's humanity had been exposed, if only for a moment, and Mike no longer found pleasure in Norm gossip. For a long time, I pined for some spiteful stories about Old Norm. It made me feel superior to criticize his nastiness, but it wasn't the hateful gossip I missed as much as I missed the social openings it allowed. With juicy stories at the ready, I always had something to talk about. I could talk to my friends, to Mike's older friends, and even to adults. Mike, of course, was the source of that wonderful social lubrication and I struggled for a while without it.

To be honest, I only knew about Old Norm from the experiences of others. Although I had seen him many times, I had only spoken to Norm Benton once. I was ten years old, and I knew nothing of his disagreeable nature. I rode my bike to a pond about half a mile past his big house just to skip rocks and search for crawdads. On my way home, I tired of peddling and walked my bike alongside his huge yard with its impressive, white, three-rail fence. I saw Norm playing fetch with his two dogs. One dog was smaller and not responsive to his commands. Norm used a tennis ball launcher to toss the balls almost the full distance of the yard. He threw them toward the end of the yard furthest from me. The dogs raced to retrieve the ball in full stride. The larger dog always got there first, picked up the ball, and ran a couple of teasing circles around the small dog before returning the ball to his master. Norm saw me watching. He purposely threw the balls to my end of the yard. The next thing I knew I had my hands full of a one-year-old Labrador pup.

The dogs bounded toward the ball, which had come to rest about twenty feet in front of me. When the young dog saw me standing by the fence, he forgot about the ball and came at me in a full burst of energy. He jumped the fence and I dropped my bike. We stood there a moment in a playful standoff. He teased, jumping from side to side with his slender front legs stretched before him and his rump held high. I outstretched my arms and spoke. It wasn't enough. Then I knelt on one knee and he wiggled toward me in timid exuberance. I grabbed his collar and stroked his head. I had a new friend on my side of the fence and, unbeknownst to me, another one on the other side.

"Well, now, you have a way with dogs, don't you?" Norm said, as he climbed over the fence. "That dog could have been long gone if you hadn't caught him. Thank you. What's your name, son?" I told him Scott Thompson and apologized for interrupting his fetch game.

"No apology necessary," he said. "You seemed to know exactly what to do with an excited puppy. You got a dog of your own?

"No, my dad says we don't have room for one."

"Who's your dad?"

"Adam Thompson," I answered.

"Oh, sure. I know your dad. Know your mom, too. Tell them hello from Norm Benton, will you?" he said, as he leashed his dog and began the walk up the lane to his big house.

I said, "I sure will." But I never did because I was afraid I would be scolded for riding my bike way out by Norm Benton's place.

7

~

Tuesday With Norm

Mike was calm, but uncertain, as he drove to work on Tuesday. He had never worried much about money or upward mobility, and having a child was a very natural occurrence. It would change his life some, but it was certainly no reason to become so anxious that you lost your perspective. Still, he wanted to do the responsible thing and, whether he liked it or not, Norm Benton had been an important part of his life. He wondered whether working full time for Norm, much like his new status as an expectant father, was simply a natural progression of things. Plus, he secretly valued Norm's observation about his leadership ability.

If he were going to become a leader of men at Norm Benton's tractor dealership, that Tuesday would not be the day of the new beginning. Rather than come in through the shop door, Mike parked up front and walked through the front door into the dealership showroom, past Norm's empty office, and down the hall to the shop. He didn't see Norm, but there was welding to do so he put on his mask and went to work. He thought Norm would invite him into his office when he was ready to talk. By midmorning he had seen nothing of Norm.

To make it easy for Norm to initiate the conversation, he went back up front to get a cup of coffee. Norm was at the front counter talking to a customer as Mike approached the coffee station, which was within an easy glance from Norm. He did not acknowledge Mike's presence. Mike poured the coffee, blew on it, took a slow sip, added some creamer, and stirred. Then he walked back to the workshop. Lunch time came and went, and Norm remained silent. The afternoon was long. Mike had only one project to complete and he tinkered with it as long as he could so that he could be available for Norm. Mike could come and go as necessary. If there was no work to do, he could leave. He had always appreciated his scheduling flexibility, but that Tuesday he chose not to use it. Finally, about a quarter until five, he decided to leave. He left through the front door and found that Norm had already gone for the day.

Molly was right. He would know what to do when the time came.

She was fixing dinner when Mike got home. Wisely, she didn't drop what she was doing and run to meet him at the door. She allowed him to reveal the day's news at his own pace. He came in through the mudroom, which adjoined the kitchen. He took off his work boots and padded into the kitchen in his stocking feet. She looked up from her chopping board and met his tight-lipped smile and an exaggerated shoulder shrug with a quizzical smile of her own.

She had considered every contingency during her day.

Would he take the job? What was the pay? Were there benefits? Would he turn it down because the money wasn't good enough? Would he tell Norm he had to sleep on it and make a counteroffer? Would he decide the job itself was not for him because managing other people was not something he wanted to do?

What happened was not something she had considered. "You will never guess what happened," he said, as he walked to the kitchen table, grabbed a chair, and sat.

"What?" she asked, chopping knife still in hand. "What did he say?"

"Not a damned thing. Old Norm was Old Norm again. Only this time, he said nothing. It was as if our earlier conversation had never happened. In fact, I think he avoided me. I gave him every opportunity to reopen the conversation. He just didn't do it."

"What? Was he just being difficult? Maybe he just wasn't ready."

"I thought about that. Or maybe I was just too eager. But to say nothing? Nothing at all? He could have told me he wasn't quite ready, that he needed more time, but he said nothing."

"I have no idea what the problem was, but I think the only way I can work with the man is if I know I can quit at any time," Mike continued. "In fact, any respect that we have for one another is based on that single truth. He gets it. I get it, and we are fine. Lose that certainty, and there would be trouble. I just cannot imagine being handcuffed to Norm's nutty behavior on a full-time basis."

She left the knife on the cutting board with the half-chopped carrot. She sat down beside him and placed her hand on his. "Good," she said.

"I love you, Molly." Mike smiled as he said it.

"That's good, too," she responded, returning his smile.

Two weeks passed, and Norm was still mum. He continued to act as if the job-offer conversation had never happened. Having made up his mind that working directly for Norm was not a good idea, Mike finally spoke up. He had nothing to lose. "You've given me lots of time to think about your job offer, Norm. What's up?"

"Do you want it or not?" Norm answered.

He had a sudden, stomach-churning desire to tell Norm that he wanted to know more about the job. He let the urge pass, and his stomach settled quickly. He answered, "No."

"Fine," Norm answered. It was never mentioned again.

8

~

Connections

Mike and Molly's first son, William, was almost five years old when I visited them in Spring Valley that year. He was a miniature Mike. The way he walked, the way he talked, and the way he loved to work with his hands, he was Mike. Dad called him William the Clone. Mom hated that. Molly just put up with it. Still, there was no doubt whose son he was. Their second child, a girl named Susan, was three years old and was the undeniable ruler of the house. It was wonderful to see them all grow and prosper.

Mike continued to split his time between the gas company and Old Norm for about three years after Ruth's funeral and the evaporating job offer. Then he opened his own welding shop and was doing very well. Norm even sent him business from time to time.

I was teaching psychology in a small college in Chanute, Nebraska, and took a long weekend to go home and catch up. Chanute was 150 miles from Spring Valley, just far enough away to make a trip home infrequent and special. We were having a beer on Mike's back deck. It was just the two of us. I asked Mike if he ever missed trading verbal swats with Old Norm.

"Oh, I still see him from time to time. He hasn't changed much. Still ornery as hell, but I still love him," he responded sarcastically. "He wanted me to do all his welding for him at a preferred rate. It would have been steady business, but I was in no mood to cut him a deal. As it is, he sends me the big stuff that his new man can't handle. I appreciate it. In fact, I've sort of come to depend on it. It works out pretty well, but I guess Dad was right about the peas and mashed potatoes, wasn't he?"

"Yea, he was. Mom was right too, you know," I added.

"About what?"

"There really are no coincidences," I said. Then I broke a promise.

"Did you ever wonder why I wasn't drafted?"

"Well, I did, but you weren't, so I didn't worry about it much. Those were tough years though. Molly still misses her brother a lot."

I was about to tell Mike something that I had never told anyone. It had been almost three years since I learned the truth and I was sworn to secrecy. Still, I always knew that I would tell Mike sometime along the way. This felt like the right time.

"Well, say nothing to Molly about this. In fact, don't say anything to anybody. I'm breaking a vow of secrecy by telling you. But there are no coincidences. Remember Peggy Stewart, my high school locker buddy? You met her at Ruth's funeral."

"Sure. I think so. Her folks have that farm north of town?"

"Yes, that's them."

"I know her dad a little. I've done some work for him."

I had mulled over Peggy's story hundreds of times. I had it memorized. I could have just blurted out that she was the reason I didn't go to war, but I didn't. I told him the story from start to finish, with every nuanced tidbit that I could remember.

"A few years ago, I ran into Peggy in the Omaha airport. I hadn't seen her in years. She was sitting in the terminal B waiting area reading. I saw her before she saw me, so I quietly sat down beside her and asked if I could carry her books.

"She was as surprised at seeing me as I was at seeing her. She was no longer quiet, plain Peggy. She was an engaging, young professional on her way to Boston for a paralegal seminar. We talked for almost twenty minutes before she had to board her flight. I learned more about her in those twenty minutes than I had in the three years as her locker neighbor. She was single and worked for an Omaha law firm. Aware that her flight would leave soon, she seemed to slip back into quiet, enigmatic Peggy. She shifted in her seat so that she could look me square in the eye and peered over the top of her glasses. Then she asked me if I had ever served in the military.

'No.' I said. 'And I do not know how I missed being drafted. My lottery number was low enough to be called, but it never was. Just lucky, I guess.'

'I have a secret. I will tell you if you never, ever speak of it to anyone.'

'I guess that is a promise I can keep.' I said nonchalantly, not knowing the magnitude of what quiet, plain Peggy was about to tell me.

'After high school, I went to business school for two years. My first job was as an administrative assistant for the

Frederick County draft board. I was there when your computer punch card came though. I trashed it.'

'You what?'

'Yep. That's what I did. It was impulsive and reckless, I know. But I always liked you and, like many people, I was fed up with the war by then, especially sitting where I was, watching people go and maybe not come back. It was odd that I even saw your card cross my desk. In fact, they instructed us not to look at the names. We were to feed the cards into a computer, which would generate a letter to the lucky draftee. But your name glared at me from the top of the stack. When I saw your card, I just took it and slipped it into a stack of papers that were to be shredded. I volunteered to do the shredding that afternoon and went home feeling pleasantly guilty. I guess it was my little way of protesting the war. You are the only person who knows this. Can you take it to your grave?' she asked with a familiar, quiet smile.

"I smiled at Peggy in disbelief for at least ten stunned seconds. 'Of course, I can and thank you, thank you, thank you!'

"I wanted to hug her, but I didn't. We talked and laughed for a few moments, mostly about the chance she had taken. We exchanged addresses and phone numbers, and she was off to Boston. I've called her only once, but I've sent her a Christmas card every year since."

"Damn, that is a story! Amazing, really." Mike seemed full of questions that he did not ask.

"Isn't it? Seems we are connected to people in ways that we cannot imagine."

"Sometimes in spite of ourselves," Mike mused.

William the Clone came to the screen door and announced that supper was ready. As we went inside, Mike said, "Damn, you surprised me. I was afraid you were going to tell me you were going to get hitched."

"Fear is a wish, brother. Fear is a wish," I said.

9

~

Margie's Tavern

Margie Larson was a full-bodied, blond lady of about fifty. She wasn't fat, just a person who would never be called petite. She loved to talk. She had a little bit of knowledge about just about everything and loved to share what she knew. Sometimes her reflections were serious. Other times they were farcical renditions of the truth as Margie knew it, which made her a born tavern owner. She was fun and witty and could size you up in a shuffle-board minute. She mentally sorted her customers into four different categories of approval. In descending order of affection, they were worth knowing, worth serving, worth keeping a close eye on, and unworthy.

Margie's Tavern, which was 15 miles from campus, allowed me to adjust to the difference between my Spring Valley home and my new place in the world. I had adapted to my associate professorship at Chanute College quite well. Still, there were times when I longed for a simpler time.

That's why I hung out at Margie's Tavern sometimes. It gave me a chance to escape academia. I think Margie considered me worth knowing.

Rex, Margie's husband, had a pest extermination business, so he was seldom around. Margie was the bartender, the custodian, the bouncer, and a standup comedian all in one. This off-the-beaten-path tavern was in a small unincorporated village called Georgia. It was not a college-kid hangout, which made it a comfortable place for me to unwind. I seldom had more than two beers, but I always had at least one repeatable Margie story to share the next day. She was famous for conversation-stopping remarks, like her take on opossums.

A bachelor farmer named Sammy sat one stool away from me at the bar complaining about the possums that were overrunning his place. "I don't know where they are coming from, but they stink, and they are driving my dogs crazy. My Lab got one of the ugly buggers and brought it right into my kitchen through the back door. Dropped it at my feet. I picked it up by the tail and threw it into the backyard to bury later. The damned thing got up and ran away. Just like that. Ran away. They say those critters will play dead for up to 45 minutes."

Margie was washing beer glasses. She looked up from the sink and joined the conversation.

"Sure, they can. That's why they call them possums.

Sammy and I shared a questioning glance. He said nothing.

I said, "Gosh, Margie, I always thought that we use the phrase 'playing possum' because possums play dead so well, not the other way around." I smiled when I said it.

"Nope, it's biblical," she responded. "God told Noah to take two of every kind of animal on the boat, one male and one female. He herded them possums onboard just behind the hedgehogs and the squirrels. All was fine until them cagey possums saw the tigers. They took one look at those big cats and dropped over dead. Noah was 600 years old at the time, but in all those years he had never seen an animal pretending to be dead. He stooped to pick up them dead varmints so he could toss them overboard, but God whispered to him, 'Noah, stop. They are not dead. They are just fooling you.' Now, the ancient Hebrew word for someone who plays tricks on you was possum. So, that's what Noah called them. Actually, he called them damned possums, but God wouldn't have it, so possums is the name that stuck.

Margie finished drying a glass and turned to place it on the back bar. Sammy muttered under his breath, "Dumb, like a fox, that one." And that she was.

I introduced Sally to Margie's. Sally was an English professor originally from North Carolina. We met when our professional paths crossed at Chanute College. We had been dating for a couple of months when I invited her to my special hideout. That night Margie was wearing a navy-blue sweatshirt inscribed with scripture. In bold-faced, gold type, it read "Be still, and know that I am God." The scriptural reference, Psalms 46:10, was printed alongside the passage in type too small to notice. The sweatshirt message fit Margie perfectly. On one hand, it demonstrated her wonderful dry wit. On the other, it announced to her clientele that she was in charge. Her hard-nosed persona was simply a barkeeper's tactic. She was a kind person who put on a veneer of gruffness to keep the peace in Margie's Tavern. We regulars were given permission see to behind her veil of intentional sternness because she knew and trusted us. She usually held newcomers at bay for a while. Sally was an exception. They hit it off right away. It was clear immediately that there was more to their playful chemistry than the comfortable presence of a mutual friend. They were soul mates. Sometimes that happens. Two people, from drastically different settings, connect in a special, almost-sacred way at their first meeting. Margie was a small-town tavern owner. Sally was an English professor from North Carolina. They clicked, and I enjoyed watching it happen.

"Well, now, who is this lovely lady, Professor," Margie said, as she approached our booth with a couple of Budweiser coasters in hand.

"Margie, please meet Sally," I responded. "She's a good friend of mine and I just thought it was high time that I introduced her to Margie's Tavern."

"Sort of a dry run before you introduce her to your parents, right?" Margie didn't wait a moment to tease her way into the conversation.

I laughed out loud. "You are my mother, Margie. Adopted, but my mom none the less."

"Nice to meet you, Margie," Sally said. "I love your sweatshirt."

"Why, thank you. Aren't you sweet? My husband gave it to me. He dared me to wear it to church. I told him I knew he loved me because I am a wild-eyed rebel, but wearing this to church would be pressing my luck. What can I get you guys?"

"I want a sweatshirt like that one," Sally kidded.

"Would you wear it to church?"

"I don't have a church. Could I wear it to your church?"

"Sure, but you'd have to do it in January. We shut this place down for a month in January and go to New Zealand. You and that sweatshirt would cause a stir and I would just as soon not be here for it," Margie said.

"Two drafts and a plate of turkey fries," I interrupted. Margie seldom made it to Omaha, let alone New Zealand. It would not be the last time I felt compelled to alter the course of their conversation. Part of their affection for one another was a shared sense of the ridiculous. Their banter could become endless as each of them tried to top the other with the last absurd thought.

Sally had never eaten fried turkey testicles. In fact, she admitted that she had a tough time even envisioning a turkey testicle, but she didn't wince when the plate of heavily breaded morsels arrived at the table. Other people might have fussed some just because they thought it was expected of them. Not Sally. Pretention was not her way. It was as alien to her as professional ambition was to my dad.

While Sally genuinely liked Margie, she was curious about my choice of Margie's Tavern as my clandestine retreat. She didn't ask me how I found the place. She asked me why. I told her it just felt like home. Then I explained further. My family didn't frequent taverns. I never saw Mom take a drink, and I don't think I saw my dad with a beer in his hands more than twice. By feeling at home, I meant I was comfortable around the people, people who were not openly ambitious. As an associate professor in a small, liberal arts college, I was surrounded by fellow academics who were trying to get published or get promoted or get invited to a more prestigious school or even become tenured where they were. I was uncomfortable with their unapologetic preoccupation with those markers of success. After all, I had grown up in a home almost devoid of professional ambition. You made a living to live, and the things that you were passionate about had nothing to do with trying to be somebody or be better than somebody. I guess Old Norm was the only person I knew who demonstrated a barefaced need to outshine you.

Sally never truly understood my relaxed attitude toward my teaching career until I took her home to meet my family about a year later. Dad had a lofty-sounding new position. Because he knew everyone for miles around and most people liked him, the county commissioner thought he would be the perfect man for a newly legislated government job. He was the noxious weed supervisor for Fredrick County. He explained the job to Sally. He told her about the harm weeds can do to the environment and to livestock. He talked about choke weed, thistles, poison hemlock, Russian knapweed and Asiatic witchweed. He enjoyed sharing his knowledge. But those of us who knew him thought that the job seemed an unlikely match for Dad. He drove his government pickup around the county looking for noxious weeds in roadside ditches and along fence lines and, when he spotted them, he notified landowners that it was their responsibility to control the weeds. Now, learning all he could about weeds was fun for him. He was a student of many things. Telling farmers, most of whom were his friends, that they had to spray or do a controlled burn to arrest the weeds was a disagreeable task. He also didn't like patrolling country roads in a conspicuous little white pickup with a State Department of Agriculture seal on both doors. I thought that he would be working somewhere new sometime soon. Later, I told Sally what I thought and a little about his varied employment history.

Sally began to understand, and we were right to assume that Dad would find some of his new duties hard to swallow. We were wrong to assume that he would not stick with it. The part of the job that he liked revealed a side of him that the family had glimpsed but never appreciated. He was a good teacher and he loved to share his knowledge. He didn't lecture. He simply talked. He was never an enforcer. He simply talked. He talked about weeds and their negative impact. In time, he was invited to speak at co-op meetings and Lions Club meetings and other civic gatherings. He was as unpretentious and laid back in front of an audience as he was when he chatted over the hood of his pickup with

a farmer. He simply talked. The state provided a profession-
ally produced slideshow and a script for such occasions. He
never used the script. He used the images to complement
his easy conversation. Uncomfortable with bureaucratic
adornment, he refused to wear the official khaki shirt with
the Department of Agriculture seal on the pocket. A freshly
ironed plaid shirt with the sleeves rolled up with two neat
folds suited him fine.

There were times when his easy manner didn't smooth
the way. He told us about one such meeting. Dad hardly
had time to step out of the pickup before Abner Van Dyke
confronted him. "I seen you driving slow along my fence
row and figured you was going to stop. I got to tell you
right up front that what you are doing is a crock, and I don't
much like no government agency telling me to take care
of something that I been taking care of for years. Weeds is
weeds. Always been weeds. Always going to be weeds. Just
got to work around them."

"You are absolutely right, Abner," Dad responded.
"And I can tell by looking at your place that you have been
doing a darn good job of it. But you do have a little poison
hemlock growing down there that I thought you might
want to know about."

"Poison hemlock?"

"Yea. I got a picture of it. Let me show you," Dad said,
as he pulled out his three-ring binder, laid it flat on the hood
of the pickup, and opened it to the hemlock picture. Abner
looked, and Dad turned the page to a picture of a bloated,
dead cow whose last supper was that noxious weed. "That's
what it'll do. Sometimes in fifteen minutes or less."

"I don't have no livestock," Abner snapped.

"No, but your neighbors do," Dad replied quickly. "We
have to work together on this. It is in everyone's best interest. Look what happened in Pennsylvania. They started a

similar program five years ago and, because everybody got on board, poison hemlock has gone the way of polio and smallpox."

"So, what are you going to do, write me a damned citation or something?"

"Abner, it's more of an invitation than a citation. We'd like you to join us in our attempt to get rid of this stuff. Would you do that?"

"What if I don't?"

"I don't know for sure," Dad lied. "You'd be the first person to turn me down. Think about it, will you?" He handed Abner a citation, got back in the pickup, offered a friendly wave, and drove away. Gamesmanship didn't come naturally to Dad, but he learned quickly. We were surprised that he was thriving in what appeared to be just another stop along his long road of false starts. Mom was as upbeat as we had ever seen her.

"Touchy business at times, I guess," Sally said.

"Yes, at times. What's your daddy do, Sally?"

"He was in the Army for thirty years. After he retired, he and Mom opened a bed and breakfast place in Asheville, North Carolina. He died about three years ago. Mom still runs it, though I won't be surprised if she sells it soon."

"So, you've moved around a lot?" Dad asked.

"Some, but I got to spend all of my high school years in one spot. That was a good thing. That was in Raleigh."

"So, how is Nebraska agreeing with you?"

"Oh, fine. I like it here. There is just one thing that bothers me," Sally said with a concerned smile on her face.

"What's that?"

The two seconds between his question and her answer were interminable. I knew the look on her face. I also knew that it was way too soon to tease him about his new job.

"There are too darn many weeds," she said.

I was wrong. Dad roared with laughter. Mom smiled confidently. It seemed that my childhood family had gone missing.

Mike, Molly, William the Clone, and baby-sister Susan joined us for supper. That's when Dad told us about the fun he had telling Old Norm that he had to do something about his noxious weeds.

10

~

Complex Norm

"So, Sally, how did you meet this guy? Mike asked. It was fun to have everyone together, and Sally fit in like a beloved first cousin, though her forthright personality unnerved me more than once. "Well, it wasn't easy," she answered.

"Actually, we first met through a mutual student," Sally continued. "I was her advisor, and she wanted to drop a class to reduce her workload for the semester. Scott's class was her chosen drop, and I gave him a courtesy call to tell him. I told him that I was afraid his introductory psychology class would soon be a student short. He gave me a response that I'll never forget."

"Really, what was that?"

"He told me that fear is a wish. Twice."

Mike blurted a quick, loud hoot. Dad's proud chuckle lingered well past Mike's hoot. Mom smiled. We all laughed because Sally thought our "curious utterance," as she called it, was worth remembering. We laughed, too, because we never thought of ourselves as curious. It was fun to have someone think so.

"I understood what he meant, but it was an unusual thought," Sally explained. "I decided I wanted to meet him. So, I managed an introduction at a faculty mixer and here we are."

"Wait a minute! You managed our introduction? You stalked me?" I kidded.

"No, it wasn't stalking. I just wanted to see who you were. I was afraid that someone with your wisdom would be a wrinkled-up, old wizard of some kind."

Though I teased my way past this revelation, I was genuinely surprised. I had incorrectly assumed that our meeting was a total coincidence. I had no idea that our family's sarcastic truism had drawn her to me. I was glad she liked it, but I flinched at my own innocence and her calculated resourcefulness, which I eventually chalked up to creativity rather than cunning.

"That's one of Dad's favorites," Mike explained.

"Yes, he's the wise one," I confessed. Sally smiled, and Susan spilled her glass of water. Molly cleaned it up quickly and assured her that little mistakes like that happen to the best of us.

"Speaking of little mistakes," Dad said. "I had to tell Old Norm he had some bad weeds on his place."

"No kidding! How did that go?" Mike asked.

"Well, ultimately he agreed to take care of the problem, but it took a while to get there. The man simply cannot help himself. First, he gave me that stupid upside-down smile and told me he had wondered whether I would have nerve enough to check out his place, especially since he gave you, Mike, so much business."

"He said that? Just like him to start a conversation with a threat. Predictable, I suppose, but still annoying as hell, isn't he?" Mike said.

"I slid right by the threat and went straight for the truth. I said that I assumed if you were welding for him, you must do really good work because I knew his reputation for excellent customer service. Then I mentioned how extremely proud I am of you."

"Didn't stop him, did it?"

"Nope. I asked him to get in the pickup so we could take a little ride to show him what I was talking about. He hesitated a moment, but got in. I could tell he was thinking about his next move, so I started talking about the perils of choke weed and how he had a stand of it on his fence line that would choke a horse. What's worse, it could spread to the neighboring field and intermingle with the soybeans. It was a short ride. I pulled up right alongside the fence line so that he would not have to get out of the truck to see the tangle of choke weeds. Then he changed the subject."

"He asked me how long I had had this job. I told him long enough. Then he asked me how long I thought I would be able to stick with it and reminded me of my own reputation. That is, a reputation for not staying with one job for very long."

"That son of a bi . . . biscuit." Mike hissed, stuttering through a midthought correction for the sake of the kids.

"What did you say to that and what the heck was your little mistake? Maybe that you didn't strangle him with a length of fresh choke weed?" I asked.

"I laughed and told him my reputation is well deserved. Then I said nothing for a long while, probably about five minutes as we drove back to his big house. He knew I was angry. As he reached for the pickup door handle, I answered his question. I told him that I was unsure how long I would stick with this job but that he could be sure that it would be long enough for me to enforce the citation I was about to give him. I told him that fact was as certain as the green on his John Deere tractors. I got out my clipboard and wrote him up."

"And your mistake?" I asked.

"I shouldn't have let him get to me. When you wrestle with a pig, he likes the mud far more than you do."

"You are forgiven. Believe me, you are forgiven," Mike sympathized.

Sally could not contain herself. "Who in the hell is Old Norm?" she asked.

I could not answer. No easy summary of Norman E. Benton was possible. We knew he was a man who loved his wife and his dogs as much as the next guy. Still, he was so antagonistic. Was he the town tormentor, the town benefactor, a despised rich man, a misunderstood curmudgeon with a kind heart hidden behind layers of insecure bluster? Or, was what seemed to be intrinsic meanness well-camouflaged self-sacrifice? That is, perhaps his goal was to demonstrate that life could be difficult, and he was willing to instruct us at the expense of his own good reputation. If that was the case, he was an excellent teacher. I could not answer.

Dad finally spoke. "He is a man who loves to find your buttons and push them. He is a heat-seeking insult waiting to happen. Why? I have no idea. But, we all sort of enjoy his orneriness."

Sally sat back in her chair. "Why don't you just stand back far enough so he can't see your buttons?"

"Tough to do in a town this size," Dad concluded.

11

~

The Proposal

I asked Sally to marry me on a gorgeous Indian summer afternoon. It was a Wednesday. We stopped at an overlook point on the Platte River that wasn't far from Margie's Tavern. It was a spot cleared and maintained especially for watching the sandhill crane migration, which occurs during March along that stretch of the river. Literally, thousands of the majestic, long-necked birds rest and feed along the Platte during their northern migration. People come from far and wide to witness this perennial event. There were no birds or other people that day. Just Sally and me and the sunshine. The sun, which was headed for a lower place in the winter sky, found an October angle that blinded me when I faced it and warmed me when my back was to it. It took a moment for me to adjust our positions so that we could face one another, unhindered by the sun's autumn brilliance. I gently grasped her shoulders and moved her slightly to the left so that the sun shone across her right cheek and my left. There we stood, and I asked, "Hey, Sally. Will you marry me?"

Her ear-to-ear grin was sudden and compete. I thought it meant yes. She affirmed my suspicion when she said, "I thought you'd never ask. Yes, I will marry you." Then she kissed me, and I placed the ring box in her right hand and tenderly folded her fingers around it. Announcing news like this takes practice, so we drove straight to Margie's Tavern.

Margie took one look at us and knew something was up. We seldom visited Margie's midweek. "Well, there's my favorite friends from another world. How are things in the hallowed halls of academia, and what brings you so far from campus today?"

"We couldn't think of a better way to enjoy this wonderful fall day than to drive to Margie's," I said, as we took a window booth far away from the very noisy pinball machine. It took her about two seconds to spot the ring on Sally's finger. She spoke with her eyes. They bounced from the ring to Sally to me and then back to the ring. She raised her brows and cocked her head in an unspoken inquiry.

Sally smiled and said, "Yes, it is true. We are getting married!"

Margie's delighted scream bounced off the ceiling and silenced the room. Two overall-clad farmers spun on their bar stools to stare. The pinball player stopped playing. A pool shooter relaxed his aim midshot and looked up.

"I knew it. I knew it. When?" Margie asked in an excited half-whisper.

"Gee, Margie, we have no idea," I answered. "We've only been engaged for about twenty minutes. Give us a little time, will you?"

"Well, I'll be. You have made my day. I was talking about you guys with Rex a couple of days ago, wondering if you were going to get together. He reminded me that it was none of my business. I told him that I would worry about anybody I chose to worry about. He said nothing more. Praise the Lord, it is time to celebrate!" she said. "Beer's on me."

She returned to the bar, drew two beers for us, iced a coke for herself, grabbed two packets of beef jerky and returned to the booth. "Scooch over," she said to Sally, and she joined us off and on for the remainder of the afternoon.

I always felt a bit guilty about sharing the news of our engagement with Margie the barkeep before we told our parents. But, I'd do it again. Margie's authentic, unrestrained joy was a glowing affirmation of our decision. I will remember it as fondly and clearly as I remember the God-sent warmth of the autumn sun.

12

~

The Wedding Gift

We spent the winter months planning the wedding. Or, at least, Sally did. I had always appreciated Sally's no-nonsense approach to life, which allowed her to fit in almost anywhere and not be sidetracked by frivolous things. Planning our wedding revealed her latent interest in trifling matters. Part of it was because of my detail-oriented mom's total willingness to help plan the wedding, which would be held in Spring Valley. Still, a new Sally seemed to emerge. I hoped it was a temporary condition. I kidded with my dad about it, suggesting that I really did not care about the color of the napkins or if the punch had strawberry sherbet floating in it. He sensed the underlying concern of my forced playfulness.

"Son," he said, "Please, remember this. When you get up in the morning, remember this. When your head hits the pillow, remember this. There are times when what you don't say will be remembered with fondness for a lifetime.

This is one of those times." It was another of his common-sense nuggets. I never knew if he had them all memorized, or if he made them up on the spot. It really didn't matter. I spent the winter trying to avoid saying things that would be remembered for a lifetime because I did not say them.

Of course, Sally knew no one from Asheville, where her mother lived. Except for three far-flung college buddies, everyone she cared about was here. Her mom was not disappointed that the wedding would be in Spring Valley because she had her hands full operating the bed and breakfast on her own. She would travel to Nebraska for the big day and appreciated the vacation.

Thanksgiving and Christmas came and went. The new semester began and sped by. The guest list was honed, the church and reception hall were reserved, travel arrangements were made and confirmed, and the invitations were printed and delivered. The sandhill crane migration occurred as it had for thousands of years, and it was time to get married.

Weddings are mostly predictable. Ours was, except for one uninvited guest. Norman E. Benton sat in the back row of the church in a freshly pressed suit and a yellow tie with tiny, green tractors on it. He did not attend the reception. He just came to the wedding, exchanged a few words with Pastor Weber, and was gone. I didn't even know he had been there, although everyone else did. Dad took it in stride. Mom didn't. Planning the wedding was an all-consuming pleasure for Mom. But, her emotional investment in the event left little room for forgiving uninvited guests. She was incensed that Old Norm crashed the wedding. Dad said it didn't matter. Sally was sorry she didn't get to meet him. Mike thought it was funny. I was surprised that he came. I was flabbergasted by the contents of his envelope.

The reception was fun. Margie was there with her husband, Rex. Peggy Stewart came. I hadn't seen her since our accidental meeting in the Omaha airport and I almost excluded her from the invitation list, but I decided that if anyone deserved one, she did. I simply told Sally she was a high school friend I had kept in touch with. I told her nothing of her courageous, illicit influence on my life. I was delighted to see her and was authentically enthusiastic as I welcomed her. Maybe too enthusiastic. She took a step back, smiled, and told me not to let it go to my head because she needed an excuse to come home and visit her parents. Unassuming Peggy was not Peggy. Relaxed and patient Mom was not Mom. Sally was coming back to normal, but a vestige of wedding-planning angst still fluttered about her. Margie, however, was Margie. She placed a neatly wrapped package on the table in front of us and demanded that we open it. She said it was a gift that could not wait until tomorrow. Inside were two blue sweatshirts with gold messages printed on the front of them. Sally's was a duplicate of the one Margie had worn when they met. "Be still, and know that I am God" was perfectly Sally. Mine also bore scriptural advice. The message from Proverbs read, "To restrain her is to restrain the wind." Margie's feminist leanings were benign and packed with good intentions. Still, as we stood and held our new sweatshirts in front of us for a picture, I felt the need for masculine advice.

"Rex, when does it stop?" I asked.

He smiled, shook his head, and said, "When they sleep."

Pastor Weber enjoyed the scriptural humor as much as anyone. "I'm glad to see you have some Christian friends," he kidded. He had spent a couple of hour-long sessions with us before the wedding just to get to know us and to politely probe the depth of our affection. He was my lifelong pastor.

I liked him. Sally did too. He was one of the most unassumingly observant people I have ever met.

"We had a full house today, didn't we? Are you pleased?" he asked.

"It was a great day, Pastor. Thank you for all your help," I answered, not even remotely aware of his oblique reference to Old Norm's attendance.

"Did you notice that Norm Benton was here?"

"No kidding? Really? That's odd."

"He asked me to give you this," he said, as he handed me an envelope with my name on it. It was not addressed to Scott and Sally or Mr. and Mrs. Thompson. It was addressed to me. Pastor Weber smiled at the puzzled look on my face.

"Aren't you going to open it?" Sally asked.

"Not now," I said. Opening a surprise envelope from Old Norm had to be a shared family moment. I stuffed it in my jacket pocket and thanked Pastor Weber. We opened it together later that night.

Our honeymoon escape was planned for the next day anyway, so we were all there for the opening. Sally's mom had to be brought up to speed on Old Norm, so each of us who knew him shared a brief Old Norm story. She seemed to more fully understand when Dad finally summed it up.

"Please don't think we are unkind. Norm does some great things for this community. But, on an everyday basis, it seems that Norm's greatest pleasure is to insult you. And he's just nice enough to you along the way that you let him get away with it. Simply put, he is a pain in the neck, who sometimes redeems himself in backhanded ways. Like today, he was not invited to the wedding but came anyway. Interestingly, he came with a gift. At least I think it's a gift," Dad explained, pointing to the envelope that lay on the table before me.

I opened it. It was a check to Mr. Scott Thompson for one thousand dollars. The note with it read, "Scott, Thank you for the help with my dog. Use this for a dog of your own when the time is right. Best of luck to you and Sally."

"What in the world is he talking about? What dog?" Mom asked.

I told them the story of that long-ago bike ride past Norm's place when I had helped capture his spirited, run-away dog. "Go figure," I said. "It was not anything heroic. I simply caught his dog as he ran straight at me. Catching it was almost accidental."

Right on cue, Dad reached into his satchel of wisdom and said. "Favors least planned are favors most favored."

He was right. Spontaneous human touches are the best touches. They are unblemished kindnesses because they have not been around long enough to be tarnished by self-interest. Sally's first phone call to me, Margie's inherent hospitality, and Peggy's impulsive draft board deception all qualify. Even Mike's visit with Norm after Ruth's death was without personal motive. Oh, Pastor Weber had his reasons, but not Mike. He was along for the ride because it seemed like the right thing to do. Certainly, catching Norm's dog was an unplanned favor.

About two weeks after the wedding, Dad drove out to Norm's place for a follow-up visit to his fence line. It was clean. Norm had sprayed his weeds and mowed them close. They were reduced to brown stubble. Norm wasn't home, but Dad left an official letter of compliance in his mailbox. He also left a handwritten note. It said, "Excellent job on your fence line. It looks great. And thank you, too, for keeping an eye on my boys."